P9-BZB-903

The Little Match Girl

by Hans Christian Andersen

illustrated by Rachel Isadora

G. P. Putnam's Sons

New York

Illustrations copyright © 1987 by Rachel Isadora Turner
All rights reserved. This book, or parts thereof, may not be reproduced
in any form without permission in writing from the publisher.
G. P. Putnam's Sons, a division of The Putnam & Grosset Group,
200 Madison Avenue, New York, NY 10016.
Sandcastle Books and the Sandcastle logo are trademarks
belonging to The Putnam & Grosset Group.
First Sandcastle Books edition, 1990. Published simultaneously in Canada.
Printed in Hong Kong by South China Printing Co. (1988) Ltd.
Designed by Nanette Stevenson.
Library of Congress Cataloging in Publication Data
Andersen, H. C. (Hans Christian), 1805-1875. the little match girl.
Translation of: Lille pige med svovlstikkerne.
Summary: The wares of the poor little match girl illuminate
her cold world, bringing some beauty to her brief, tragic life.
[1. Fairy tales] I. Isadora, Rachel, ill. II. Title.
PZ8.A542Lis 1987 [Fic] 85-30082
ISBN 0-399-21336-8 (hardcover)
11 13 15 17 19 20 18 16 14 12
ISBN 0-399-22007-0 (paperback)
7 9 10 8

For
Elizabeth Gillian

It was late on a bitterly cold New Year's Eve. The snow was falling. A poor little girl was wandering in the dark cold streets; she was bareheaded and barefoot.

She had of course had slippers on when she left home, but they were not much good, for they were so huge. They had last been worn by her mother, and they fell off the poor little girl's feet when she was running across the street to avoid two carriages that were rolling rapidly by. One of the shoes could not be found at all, and the other was picked up by a boy who ran off with it, saying that it would do for a cradle when he had children of his own.

So the poor little girl had to walk on with her little bare feet, which were red and blue with the cold. She carried a quantity of matches in her old apron, and held a packet of them in her hand. Nobody had bought any from her during all the long day, and nobody had even given her a copper. The poor little creature was hungry and perishing with cold, and she looked the picture of misery.

The snowflakes fell on her long yellow hair, which curled so prettily round her face, but she paid no attention to that. Lights were shining from every window, and there was a most delicious odor of roast goose in the streets, for it was New Year's Eve. She could not forget that!

She found a corner where one house projected a little beyond the next one, and here she crouched, drawing up her feet under her, but she was colder than ever. She did not dare to go home, for she had not sold any matches and had not earned a single penny. Her father would beat her, and besides it was almost as cold at home as it was here. They had only the roof over them, and the wind whistled through it although they stuffed up the biggest cracks with rags and straw.

Her little hands were almost stiff with cold. Oh, one little match would do some good! If she only dared, she would pull one out of the packet and strike it on the wall to warm her fingers. She pulled out one. *R-r-sh-sh!* How it sputtered and blazed! It burnt with a bright clear flame, just like a little candle, when she held her hand round it.

Now the light seemed very strange to her! The little girl fancied that she was sitting in front of a big stove with polished brass feet and handles. There was a splendid fire blazing in it and warming her so beautifully, but—what happened?

Just as she was stretching out her feet to warm them, the flame went out, the stove vanished—and she was left sitting with the end of the burnt match in her hand.

She struck a new one. It burnt, it blazed up, and where the light fell upon the wall, it became transparent like gauze, and she could see right through it into the room. The table was spread with a snowy cloth and pretty china. A roast goose stuffed with apples and prunes was steaming on it. And what was even better, the goose hopped from the dish with the carving knife sticking in his back and waddled across the floor. It came right up to the poor child, and then—the match went out, and there was nothing to be seen but the thick black wall.

She lit another match. This time she was sitting under a lovely Christmas tree. It was much bigger and more beautifully decorated than the one she had seen when she peeped through the glass doors at the rich merchant's house this very Christmas. Thousands of lighted candles gleamed under its branches. And many colored pictures, such as she had seen in the shop windows, looked down at her.

The little girl stretched out both her hands toward them—then out went the match. All the Christmas candles rose higher and higher, till she saw that they were only the twinkling stars. One of them fell and made a bright streak across the sky.

Someone is dying, thought the little girl, for her old grandmother, the only person who had ever been kind to her, used to say, "When a star falls, a soul is going up to God."

Now she struck another match against the wall, and this time it was her grandmother who appeared in the circle of flame. She saw her quite clearly and distinctly, looking so gentle and happy.

"Grandmother!" cried the little creature. "Oh, do take me with you. I know you will vanish when the match goes out. You will vanish like the warm stove, the delicious goose, and the beautiful Christmas tree!"

She hastily struck a whole bunch of matches, because she did so long to keep her grandmother with her. The light of the matches made it as bright as day. Grandmother had never before looked so big or so beautiful. She lifted the little girl up in her arms, and they soared in a halo of light and joy, far, far above the earth, where there was no more cold, no hunger, and no pain—for they were with God.

In the cold morning light the poor little girl sat there, in the corner between the houses, with rosy cheeks and a smile on her face—dead. Frozen to death on the last night of the old year. New Year's Day broke on the little body still sitting with the ends of the burnt-out matches in her hand.

"She must have tried to warm herself," they said. Nobody knew what beautiful visions she had seen, nor in what a halo she had entered with her grandmother upon the glories of the New Year.